# CELEBRI
# HOLIDAYS AROUND THE WORLD

## FACTS & FUN

## FOR AGES 5-9

Written by
**Laurie Rozakis**

Illustrated by
**Bev Armstrong**

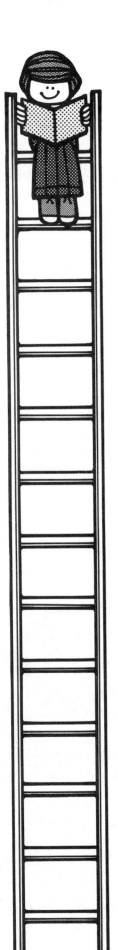

# The Learning Works

### Acknowledgement

*Sincere thanks go to all of the agencies, councils, individuals, and organizations who helped in our efforts to gather information about the holidays and festivals in this book. Special thanks go to those who shared so many memories and stories of their personal holiday experiences.*

**The Learning Works, Inc.**
P.O. Box 6187
Santa Barbara, California 93160

Library of Congress Number: 92-081915
**ISBN 0-88160-217-5**
**LW 107**

Printed in the United States of America.
Current Printing (last digit): 10 9 8 7 6 5 4

## Note to Parents and Teachers

What are celebrations? Celebrations are special days that people set aside to commemorate an important time. Some are religious, others patriotic, and still others, ethnic or cultural. Some celebrations mark a new season, and some honor an individual. Some are celebrated by many countries, while others may be observed in one small village or by a single tribe.

**Celebrate!** describes fourteen holidays and festivals from around the world. Read the description of each holiday together with your child or class. Use the related craft projects, games, recipes, and coloring pages as ways of increasing a child's understanding of the holiday. The extended activities at the end of the book offer opportunities for children to see the similarities and differences among celebrations and to learn more about other cultures and countries.

**Celebrate!** introduces young children to the wealth of cultural traditions that are an important part of the world we live in. This book invites children to see the many ways in which people around the world **Celebrate!**

# Contents

# Chinese New Year

**Chinese New Year** begins between January 21 and February 19. To get ready for the new year, families clean their houses from top to bottom. They put away sharp things like scissors and knives, so nothing will "cut" the luck of the new year. People wear new clothes and shoes to begin the year.

New year's wishes written on long scrolls are hung in homes and in store windows. Some families keep a picture of a kitchen god in their homes. Before the new year begins, they smear honey on the god's lips so he will make a sweet report about the family.

The Chinese New Year celebration ends with a parade led by a long dragon made of bamboo, paper, and silk. People hold up the dragon and make it dance and weave through the streets.

## Make a Good Luck Money Envelope

In China, the color red represents happiness and good fortune. During the Chinese New Year, children get money in red envelopes for luck in the coming year.

### What You Need

- ☐ a sheet of red paper, about 9 inches square
- ☐ tape or glue
- ☐ glitter, sequins, stickers, or other decorations

### What You Do

1. Fold one corner of the paper up to the center of the square.
2. Fold the two side corners to the center.
3. Tape or glue the side folds to make a pocket.
4. Fold the top corner down to form a flap.
5. Decorate the envelope with colorful designs.
6. Use your envelope to collect coins or fortunes.

**Celebrate!**
©1993, The Learning Works, Inc.

# Chinese New Year

**The Chinese New Year ends with a colorful parade. The dragon dance is believed to chase away bad luck.**

# Tet

The Vietnamese New Year, or **Tet**, lasts for three days. Like Chinese New Year, it begins between January 21 and February 19.

People make a fresh start for the new year by cleaning and painting their homes. They pay back any money they owe, and they avoid arguments and harsh words. People eat holiday foods like sticky rice cakes, which are cooked for at least eight hours!

The first visitor of the new year is important to a Vietnamese family. A child or other relative is sent outside just before midnight and invited to reenter a few minutes later. This is to make sure that the first visitor of the new year is one who will bring the family good luck.

Vietnamese families want to start the new year right. They hope that their preparations for Tet will bring good things in the year ahead.

## Play the Game of Da-Cau

The game of **da-cau** (*dah-COW*) is a favorite of Vietnamese children. Traditionally, it is played with a coin decorated with paper strips.

### What You Need

☐ a beanbag

### How You Play

1. Lay or drop the beanbag on top of your foot.
2. Kick the beanbag in the air. If you are practicing the game by yourself, try to catch the beanbag on your foot before it touches the ground.
3. To play with a friend, kick the beanbag back and forth in the air. Using only your feet, see how many times you and your friend can catch the beanbag before it touches the ground.

6

# Tet

**Music is part of the Tet celebration. Musicians play a Vietnamese instrument with many strings.**

# Carnival

**Carnival** is a time for parades and parties. It is celebrated six weeks before Easter in many countries around the world, including Brazil, France, Haiti, Italy, Trinidad, and the United States. The most famous American Carnival is in New Orleans, Louisiana, where the holiday is known as Mardi Gras.

During Carnival, people eat sweet, rich foods. Once Carnival is over, many people give up eating that kind of food during the six weeks until Easter.

There is a huge parade on Shrove Tuesday, the last day of Carnival. Bands, dancers and floats make their way through cheering crowds. People wear fancy masks and colorful costumes. They celebrate by throwing confetti, blowing noisemakers, dancing, and having fun.

## Make a Carnival Mask

### What You Need

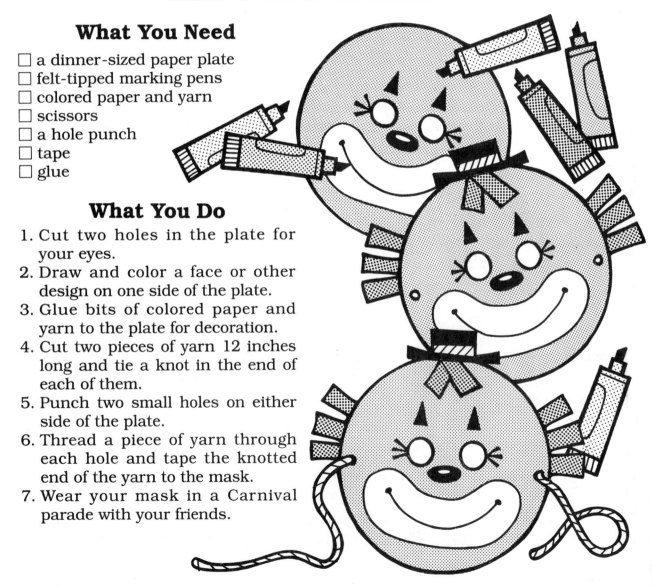

- ☐ a dinner-sized paper plate
- ☐ felt-tipped marking pens
- ☐ colored paper and yarn
- ☐ scissors
- ☐ a hole punch
- ☐ tape
- ☐ glue

### What You Do

1. Cut two holes in the plate for your eyes.
2. Draw and color a face or other design on one side of the plate.
3. Glue bits of colored paper and yarn to the plate for decoration.
4. Cut two pieces of yarn 12 inches long and tie a knot in the end of each of them.
5. Punch two small holes on either side of the plate.
6. Thread a piece of yarn through each hole and tape the knotted end of the yarn to the mask.
7. Wear your mask in a Carnival parade with your friends.

# Carnival

**Carnival is a time for celebration. People dressed in colorful costumes fill the streets.**

# Kuomboka

**Kuomboka** (*Kwahm-BOH-kah*) is a ceremony held by the Lozi people of Zambia, a country in eastern Africa. In late February or early March, heavy rains cause the Zambezi River to flood its banks. The Lozi people, who live near the banks of the river, must move to higher ground to escape the flood.

In a ceremony called the Kuomboka, the Lozis take their chief to safety in a long boat. Oarsmen steer the boat with long poles. The chief's wife has her own boat, and there is another boat for the drummers who play along the trip. The rest of the Lozis follow in canoes.

In the fall, the chief and his people return to their homes by the Zambezi River.

## Keep the Boat Afloat

### What You Need

- [ ] several empty margarine tubs
- [ ] marbles or stones
- [ ] a dishpan or basin
- [ ] water

### What You Do

1. Fill the dishpan or basin with water.
2. Float one empty margarine tub in the water.
3. Guess how many marbles or stones you can put in the margarine tub before it starts to sink.
4. Count the marbles or stones as you carefully place them, one at a time, in the margarine tub. Stop when the tub starts to sink. How close was your guess?
5. Make a Kuomboka procession of several margarine tubs. Weight each tub with marbles or stones so that it will stay afloat in the water.

**Celebrate!**
©1993, The Learning Works, Inc.

# Kuomboka

The chief of the Lozi tribe in Zambia is taken to higher ground
in a royal boat. The ceremony is called the Kuomboka.

# Noruz

**Noruz** (*No-ROOZ*) is the new year celebration in Iran. It begins on March 21 and lasts for thirteen days. Cannons and fireworks give the signal that the holiday has begun.

Iranian people wear new clothes for Noruz. They clean their homes inside and out. Children are given colored eggs and shiny new coins for the new year.

On the last day of Noruz, families go to the country for picnics. They believe being outside will bring good luck in the new year.

## Make a Sabzeh

Two weeks before Noruz, Iranian families plant a pot of fast-growing seeds called a **sabzeh** (*SOB-zuh*). The sabzeh is a symbol of good fortune and new life.

### What You Need

- ☐ a plastic berry container
- ☐ vermiculite (available at a nursery)
- ☐ fast-sprouting seeds, such as wheat grass, beans, barley, or lentils
- ☐ plastic wrap
- ☐ a small plate
- ☐ water
- ☐ sunlight

### What You Do

1. Line the berry container with plastic wrap and fill it with vermiculite, leaving about an inch at the top.
2. Sprinkle the seeds on top of the vermiculite. Use a lot of seeds to make the sabzeh thick.
3. Water the container until the soil is very moist.
4. Place the small plate under the container and put it where it will get plenty of sunlight.
5. Cover the container loosely with plastic wrap for a day or two and then remove it. The seeds should begin to sprout in a few days.
6. When your sabzeh has grown, clip the sprouts to sprinkle on a salad.

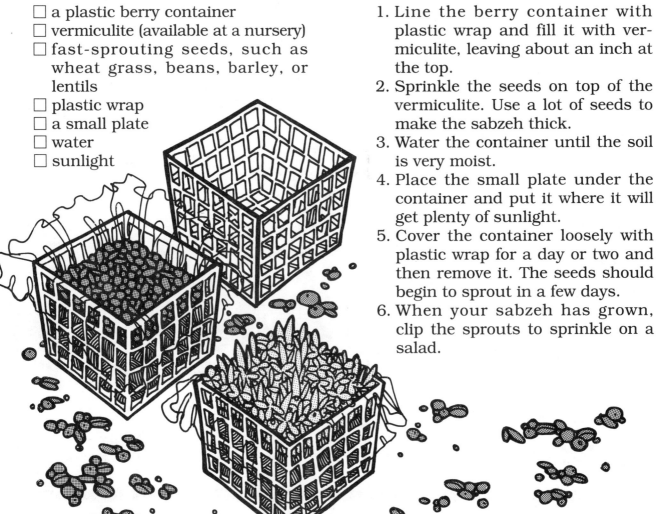

# Noruz

On the last day of Noruz, Iranian families go to the country for a picnic. Being outside brings good luck for the year ahead.

# Kodomo-No-Hi

Japanese boys and girls each have their own day of celebration during the year. Kodomo-No-Hi (*KOH-doh-moh-noh-HEE*), or Children's Day, is observed on May 5 and is a time when Japanese families honor their sons. Girls have their own special day, Hina Matsuri (*Hee-nah-MAT-soo-REE*), on March 3. On Hina Matsuri, girls display beautiful dolls in their homes and have parties.

During Kodomo-No-Hi, families fly huge carp streamers from their roofs or from tall poles in their gardens. Carp are very strong fish that swim up fast-moving streams. In Japan, the carp stands for courage.

Boys set out other symbols of strength and courage, like warrior dolls dressed in traditional costumes. For luck, boys eat sweet rice cakes wrapped in dried oak leaves.

## Make a Paper Carp

Colorful carp are made out of blue, gold, red, and yellow paper or cloth for Kodomo-No-Hi. Some carp streamers are only a few inches long, while others can be as long as a small airplane!

### What You Need

☐ a sheet of colored construction paper
☐ scissors
☐ a hole punch
☐ felt-tipped marking pens
☐ a stick or dowel about 12 inches long
☐ tape

### What You Do

1. Draw a picture of a carp on the construction paper. Use the picture of the carp on this page as a model.
2. Color designs on your carp with the marking pens.
3. Use the scissors to cut out your carp.
4. Make holes at the top and bottom of your carp with the hole punch.
5. Run the stick or dowel through the holes. Use tape to hold the fish to the stick.

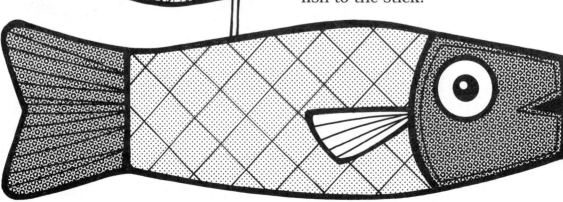

# Kodomo-No-Hi

**During Kodomo-No-Hi, families fly streamers shaped like carp. The carp is a symbol of strength and courage.**

# Urini Nal

Korean Children's Day, **Urini Nal** (*Uh-REE-nee NAHL*), was created to give children their own special day. Urini Nal is celebrated on May 5 in the Republic of South Korea.

On that day, children do not go to school. They may get in free to some museums, theaters, and zoos. There are dance performances, plays, and sporting events. Children can enter painting and writing contests, and they receive candy and small gifts from their parents.

Urini Nal is a time for Korean children to feel proud and honored.

## Play a game of Yut

**Yut** (*Yoot*) is a popular Korean game that has been played for over a thousand years. Here is a simple version of Yut for two players.

### What You Need

- ☐ Yut playing board
- ☐ 3 ice cream sticks
- ☐ 2 different game markers or beans
- ☐ felt-tipped marking pens

### What You Do

1. Make a Yut board like the one shown on this page.
2. Draw a design on one side of each ice cream stick.

### How You Play

**The object of the game** is to move your game marker around the board and back to the starting circle.

1. Place the game markers on the **Start** circle.
2. Toss the three ice cream sticks in the air.
3. Move your game marker according to how the sticks land.
   **4 spaces for 3 blank sticks**
   **3 spaces for 3 decorated sticks**
   **2 spaces for 2 decorated sticks**
   **1 space for 1 decorated stick**
4. If you land on a space where the other player has a marker, that player must go back to **Start**, and you get another turn.
5. The first player to get his or her marker back to **Start** wins the game.

# Urini Nal

**Korean children wear colorful costumes on Urini Nal.**
**They may spend a day at the park or at the zoo.**

# Green Corn Dance

The **Green Corn Dance** has been performed for hundreds of years by many Native American tribes. This ceremony is held when the corn crop is ready to harvest, sometime between May and October.

The Green Corn Dance is a time for members of the tribe to come together from far away. Long ago, special shelters were built so visitors would have a place to stay.

People give thanks for the corn crop. They settle quarrels and disagreements. In their homes, they make a fresh start by throwing away anything that is unusable or broken.

Everyone enjoys a feast with foods from the harvest. Tribe members perform dances and sing traditional songs. The Green Corn Dance is a time of great celebration.

## Bake Corn Bread

Corn bread was often cooked over a fire on a smooth stone. The bread was unleavened, or flat. Try baking two pans of corn bread. Add 1 tablespoon of baking powder to the dry ingredients of the second batter, and see the difference leavening makes in the baked breads!

### What You Need

- ☐ 1 cup of cornmeal
- ☐ 1 cup of flour
- ☐ 1 cup of milk
- ☐ 1 teaspoon of salt
- ☐ 1/4 cup of corn oil
- ☐ 8" square baking pan
- ☐ margarine to grease the pan
- ☐ mixing bowl
- ☐ large spoon

### What You Do

1. Preheat the oven to 400°.
2. Grease the pan with margarine.
3. Mix the cornmeal, flour, and salt.
4. Add the milk and the oil to the dry mixture and stir.
5. Spoon the mixture into the pan.
*6. Place the pan in the oven to bake for 20 minutes.
*7. Remove the pan from the oven when it is done.
8. Cool slightly before you cut the bread into squares.

* Adult help needed

# Green Corn Dance

**A traditional game is played during the Green Corn Dance.
Teams of men and women try to hit a target on a tall pole.**

# Festa dos Tabuleiros

**Festa dos Tabuleiros** (*FES-tah dos TAB-u-LAIR-os*), or the Feast of Trays, is a festival held every other July in the town of Tomar, Portugal. Festa dos Tabuleiros has been celebrated in Tomar for hundreds of years.

In this festival, as many as a hundred young women dressed in white walk through the streets of the town. On her head, each woman wears a basket piled with loaves of bread, paper flowers and stalks of wheat, all topped by a paper crown. It is not easy to balance this basket, because it is as high as the woman is tall! Someone walks next to each woman to be sure her headpiece does not fall over.

The procession, which includes oxen, a brass band, and drummers, goes to the local church. There, the loaves of bread and other food are given to the poor.

## Help Those In Need

Ask your parents, your friends, or your class to help you collect things to share with people in need.

**Canned Food**          **Toys**          **Clothing**

**Books**          **Furniture**          **Money**

20

# Festa dos Tabuleiros

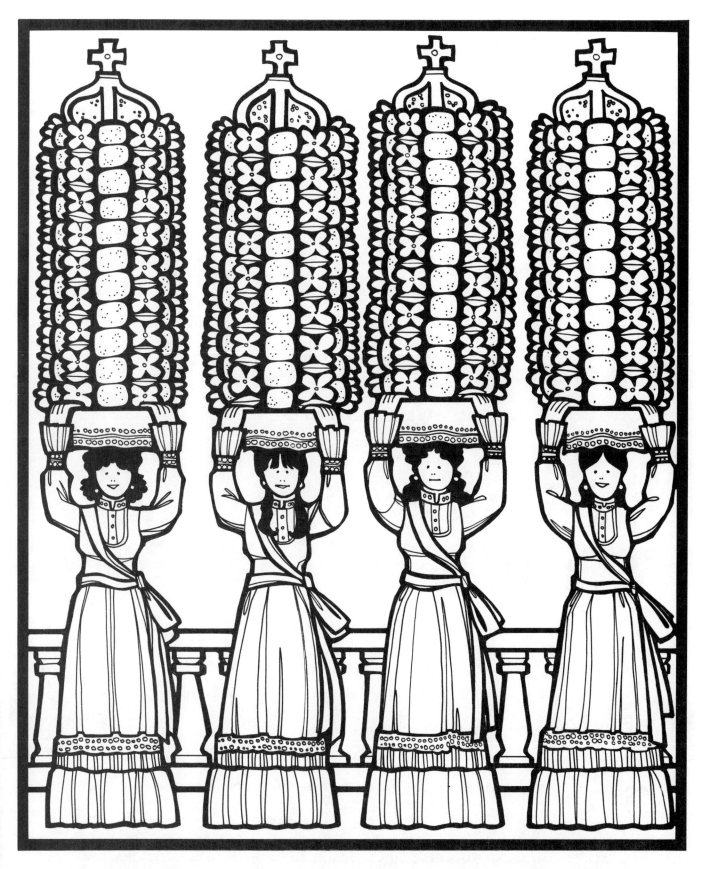

**Women carry trays of bread on their heads during Festa dos Tabuleiros. After the festival, the food is given away.**

# Odwira

**Odwira** (*Oh-dzwee-RAH*), is celebrated in September by the Akuapim people of Ghana in western Africa. Odwira is a time for family members to gather. Those who live far away return home for the holiday.

Everyone cooks delicious meals for Odwira. Parents send children with food to the homes of friends and family, where they are invited in to eat. Children like to go to homes where they know their favorite foods have been prepared!

During Odwira, arguments must be settled. The people who have argued drink from the same cup and eat from the same plate to show that they have settled their dispute.

At the end of Odwira, drums sound, and people gather to listen to the elders of the tribe. They talk about what has happened during the previous year.

## Cook Fufu

One of the special Odwira dishes is **fufu** (*foo-foo*), balls made of mashed yams. Fufu is usually served with soup or stew.

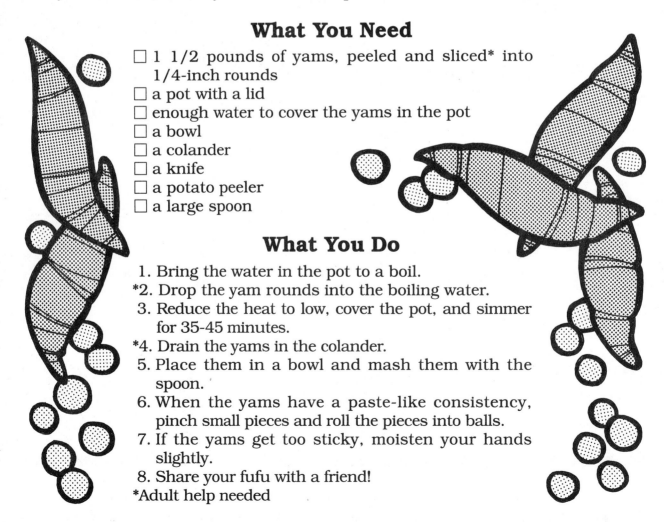

### What You Need

- ☐ 1 1/2 pounds of yams, peeled and sliced* into 1/4-inch rounds
- ☐ a pot with a lid
- ☐ enough water to cover the yams in the pot
- ☐ a bowl
- ☐ a colander
- ☐ a knife
- ☐ a potato peeler
- ☐ a large spoon

### What You Do

1. Bring the water in the pot to a boil.
*2. Drop the yam rounds into the boiling water.
3. Reduce the heat to low, cover the pot, and simmer for 35-45 minutes.
*4. Drain the yams in the colander.
5. Place them in a bowl and mash them with the spoon.
6. When the yams have a paste-like consistency, pinch small pieces and roll the pieces into balls.
7. If the yams get too sticky, moisten your hands slightly.
8. Share your fufu with a friend!
*Adult help needed

# Odwira

**Odwira ends with the chief speaking under a brightly colored umbrella. His clothes are made of a beautiful woven cloth.**

# Sukkot

**Sukkot** (*Soo-KOAT*) is a Jewish harvest holiday celebrated in the fall of the year. During Sukkot, many Jewish families build a small booth called a **sukkah** (rhymes with *book-a*).

The roof of the sukkah is made of green branches. Children decorate the sukkah with flowers, fruit, and vegetables. During Sukkot, many families place a table inside the sukkah and eat their meals there.

When families build the sukkah, they remember a time thousands of years ago when the Jewish people wandered in the desert for forty years to escape slavery. When the wanderers needed to rest, they built huts like the sukkah to stay in.

Sukkot is a happy festival. Children enjoy decorating the sukkah. Families and friends visit and share the fruits of the harvest.

## Make a Sukkah

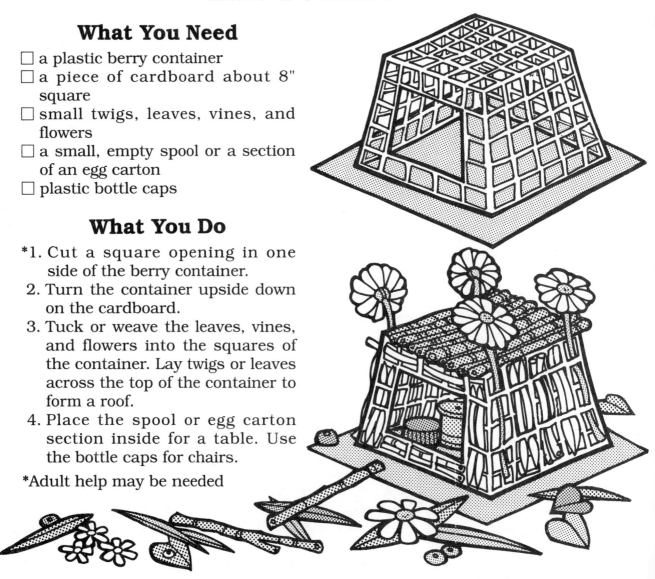

### What You Need

☐ a plastic berry container
☐ a piece of cardboard about 8" square
☐ small twigs, leaves, vines, and flowers
☐ a small, empty spool or a section of an egg carton
☐ plastic bottle caps

### What You Do

*1. Cut a square opening in one side of the berry container.

2. Turn the container upside down on the cardboard.

3. Tuck or weave the leaves, vines, and flowers into the squares of the container. Lay twigs or leaves across the top of the container to form a roof.

4. Place the spool or egg carton section inside for a table. Use the bottle caps for chairs.

*Adult help may be needed

# Sukkot

**During Sukkot, children enjoy decorating the sukkah with fresh vegetables, fruits, and flowers.**

# Kwanzaa

**Kwanzaa** (*KWAHN-zah*) is celebrated by many African-Americans. It lasts for seven days, from December 26 to January 1. During Kwanzaa, families come together to celebrate their African heritage.

Candles are lit in a candleholder called a **kinara** *(kee-NAH-rah)*. Each day of Kwanzaa has a special meaning, such as working together, sharing, or creating beauty. By the end of Kwanzaa, children have learned all of its special meanings. Then they get gifts that are usually African or handmade.

On the last day of Kwanzaa, family and friends enjoy a feast. They might sing songs, play music, and share stories of their family history.

## Make a Mkeka

A **mkeka** *(muh-KAY-kuh)*, or place mat, is one of the seven traditional symbols of Kwanzaa. An ear of corn is placed on the mkeka for each child in the family. Make your own mkeka in the traditional Kwanzaa colors of black, green, and red.

### What You Need

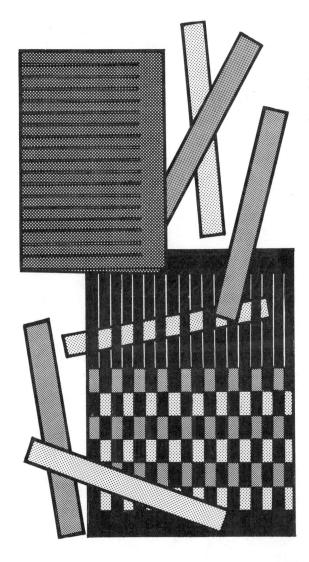

- ☐ one sheet each of black, green, and red construction paper
- ☐ ruler
- ☐ pencil
- ☐ scissors
- ☐ tape

### What You Do

1. Fold the sheet of black paper in half as shown.
2. Use the ruler to draw lines from the fold to 1 inch from the end of the paper. Make the lines about 1/2 inch apart.
3. Cut the paper on the lines you have drawn.
4. Cut lengthwise strips about 1 inch wide from the red and green paper.
5. Weave the red and green strips in and out of the slits on the black paper.
6. Tape the ends of the strips down to hold them in place. Trim the edges.

# Kwanzaa

**The seven Kwanzaa symbols are fruits and vegetables, a mkeka, a kinara, candles, corn, gifts, and a holiday cup.**

# Fiesta

**Fiestas** are celebrated in Mexico, Central America, and South America. A fiesta may be held in honor of a saint, a religious holiday, or a national holiday.

Fiesta in a small Mexican village might begin at dawn with the sound of church bells and fireworks. Some villagers go to church in the morning. Later, many people stroll through the streets, where candy, toys, and souvenirs are for sale. People celebrate fiesta by singing, dancing, playing games, and holding colorful parades.

A favorite fiesta game is the **piñata** (*peen-YAH-tah*), a hollow container decorated with tissue and filled with candy and small toys. The piñata is hung from the ceiling or from a tree. Blindfolded children take turns trying to break the piñata with a stick. When the piñata finally bursts, the children gather the toys and treats that were hidden inside.

## Make Fiesta Clay Figures

### What You Need

- ☐ modeling clay
- ☐ toothpicks
- ☐ newspaper to work on

### What You Do

1. For the body of your figure, make a ball of clay about 3 inches in diameter. Roll it sideways into a cylinder and set it upright on the newspaper.
2. Make a ball about the size of a walnut for the head. Attach it to the body, smoothing the neck with your fingers.
3. For the arms, make two small rolls and attach them to the body.
4. Form a clay hat, some shoes, or a nose. You can also carve details into the clay with a toothpick.
5. Make a collection of figures to create a fiesta scene.

# Fiesta

**Over here! Over there! A fiesta piñata is filled with candy and toys. When it breaks, everyone gets treats.**

# Powwow

**Powwow** is an important event for many American Indian tribes. Powwows and other ceremonies are held year-round by tribes in different parts of the United States. Food, singing, drums, and dancing are all part of Powwow.

Powwow brings tribes and families together. Dancers wear colorful costumes decorated with feathers and beads, like their ancestors wore. There are contests for the best dancers and singers. Children play games and listen to stories.

Powwow is a time when ancient traditions are passed down from grandmothers and grandfathers to young people. It is a time for members of a tribe to be together and to feel proud of their heritage.

## Make a Powwow Drum

### What You Need

- [ ] an empty oatmeal box with a lid
- [ ] construction paper or art paper
- [ ] glue
- [ ] tape
- [ ] scissors
- [ ] tape measure
- [ ] felt-tipped marking pens
- [ ] beads, bells, feathers, ribbon, string, and other odds and ends

### What You Do

1. Using the tape measure, measure around the oatmeal box. Then measure the box from top to bottom.
2. Cut the paper in a rectangle that is the same height as the box and 1/2 inch more in length.
3. Use the marking pens to make colorful designs on the paper.
4. Wrap the paper around the box and glue it where the ends overlap.
5. Glue or tape feathers, strings of bells or beads, ribbons, and other decorations to the box.
6. Beat a rhythm on your colorful powwow drum!

**30**

# Powwow

**Native American dancers wear beautiful costumes.
Sometimes the dancers dress like birds or animals.**

**Celebrate!**
©1993, The Learning Works, Inc.

# Learning About Other Countries

Here are some fun ways to learn more about other countries.

**Using a world map, find some of the countries that are named in this book.**

**Draw pictures of flags of other countries.**

**Listen to tapes or records with songs of other countries.**

**Draw a picture of yourself celebrating one of the holidays in this book.**

**Visit a museum to see costumes, crafts, tools, animals, and other things from many countries.**

**Visit someone who has a collection of stamps, coins, dolls, or postcards from around the world.**

**Read books about people in other places around the world.**

AFRICA
PERU

**Talk about how the holidays you celebrate are like the holidays in this book.**

**Eat at a restaurant that serves food from another country.**